The ABCs of Cookies

By P.J. Shaw
Illustrated by Tom Leigh

A is for apron, which matches this hat.

2

B is for butter, and...

D is for dishes.

E is for eggs, and...

F is for flour.

H is for honey.

K is for krispies you put on the top.

L is for **lemon** juice.

N is for nutmeg.

O is for oven.

P is for pan. (But first put your glove on!)

RAISINS

R is for raisins, golden and sweet.

S is for **sprinkles**.
And now…

18

Time to eat!

U-m-m-m-m is the way
a warm cookie tastes.

W is whipped cream to swirl on the top.
Or give a quick squeeze and then...

X marks the spot!

Z is for zero—they're all in your tummy!

S is for School!

By P.J. Shaw
Illustrated by Joe Mathieu

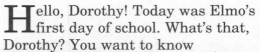

Hello, Dorothy! Today was Elmo's first day of school. What's that, Dorothy? You want to know what it's like on the very first day of school? Elmo will tell you.

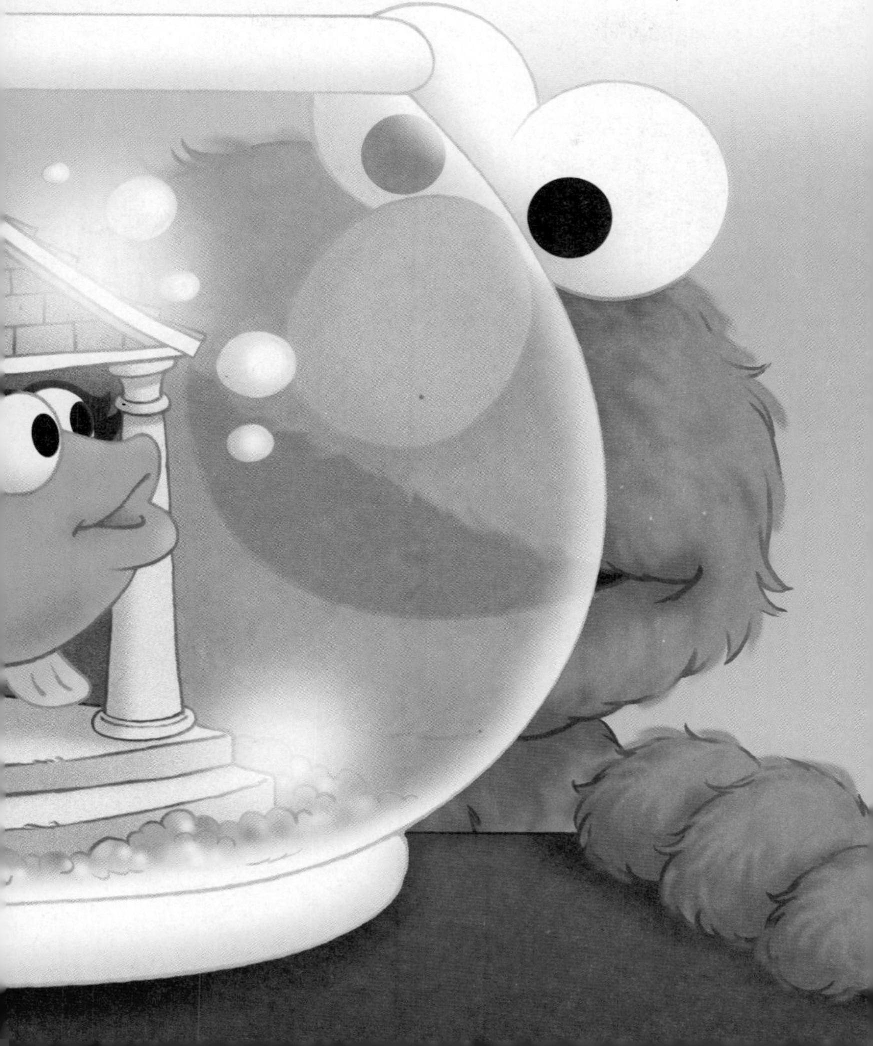

Just getting there is an **adventure**!

Some monsters wonder what to do on the first day of school.

So it helps to have a buddy. Furry ones are fun!

At school, you might feel a little lonely now and then.

But a smile helps you make new friends.
A smile—and some crayons!

¡Hola! That means hello in Spanish.

On the first day of school, a little fish can get homesick... so bring a picture for company. Guess what? Elmo brings a picture of Dorothy!

On the first day of school you see lots of new faces.

Lots of *friendly* faces! Yay!

43

The *end* of the first day of school is exciting, too.

Did you miss Elmo today?

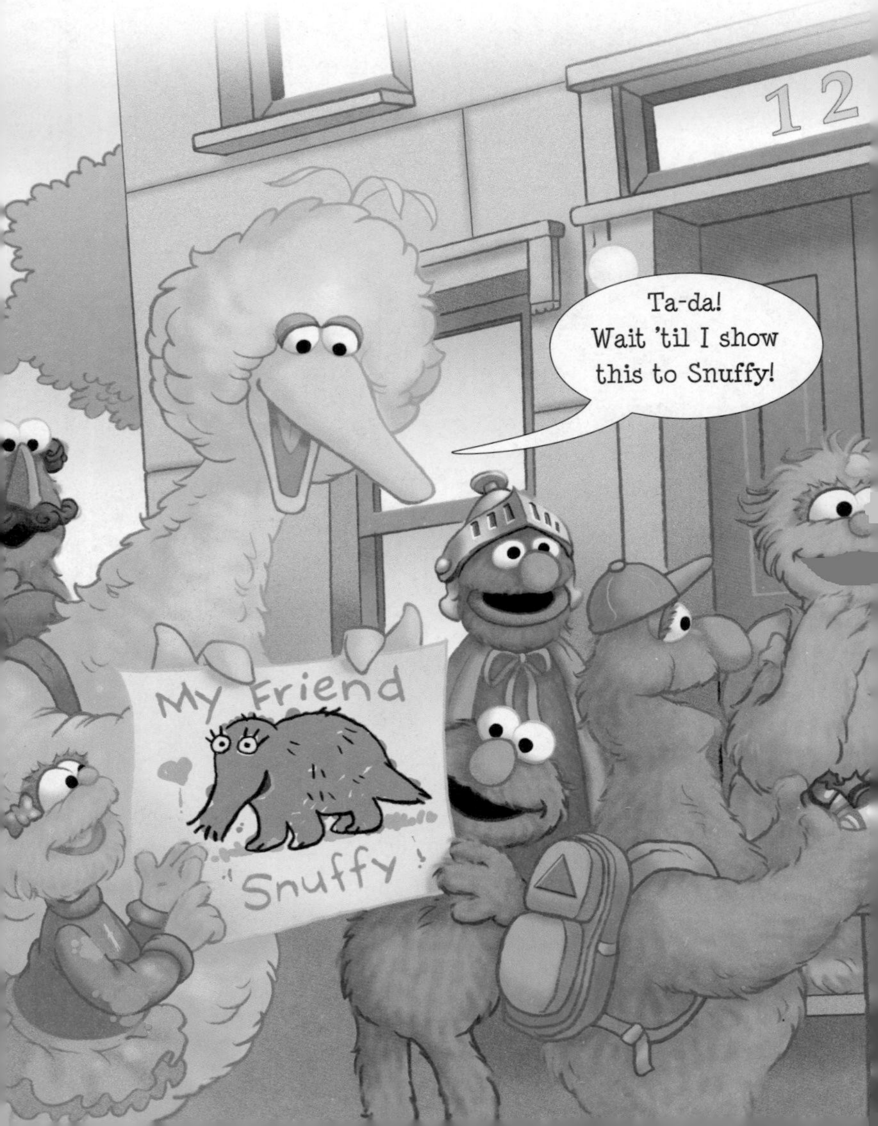
12
Ta-da!
Wait 'til I show this to Snuffy!
My Friend Snuffy!

It's a good time
for sharing what you've learned…

...with a friend!